Stories

Moshum & Kokum

Told Me

Stories Moshum & Kokum Told Me

by Arnold J. Isbister

WINGATE PRESS

Stratford, ON

STORIES MOSHUM & KOKUM TOLD ME

Library and Archives Canada Cataloguing in Publication

ISBN number: 0-9735977-6-3

Layout design by Wingate Press
Edited by Stacey Lynn Newman
Cover Design by Stacey Lynn Newman
Cover Image - "Healing Ceremony" by Arnold J. Isbister

Published by:
Wingate Press
Stratford, ON
Canada
publisher@wingatepress.com
www.wingatepress.com

It is important to protect the environment and to use natural resources responsibly. This book is printed on 100% ancient-forest-free paper (100% post-consumer recycled) and processed chlorine-and-acid-free.

Printed in Canada by Blitzprint, Calgary, AB

Contents

This goes to my Mother & Dad (Pansy & Paul) who I call Moshum & Kokum and to my kids Michelle, Warren, Chelsea and Carolyn who will be grandparents one day. They will relive their days through their children. My life and stories are not complete without my most treasured and trusted friend, Karen my beloved wife who is always beside me through troubled times.

Also a thank you to all my relatives, friends and community whose rich culture will endure through these stories based on fact. Finally but not least I sincerely thank Mrs. Stacey Newman who saw something, believed in my writing and decided to take the chance and publish them. Without her there would be nothing.

INTRODUCTION

From the Publisher

Arnold Isbister first approached us with just one of his short stories, *Going Home*. It was this short story that prompted us to request additional pieces about his Moshum & Kokum. We were immediately moved by the *sound* of Arnold's characters, their individual voices, the realistic and beautiful dialogue, and by the profound emotion present in each of his stories.

The seven stories contained in *Stories Moshum & Kokum Told Me* are a window into a private, familial world filled with a rich and fantastic history that is passed from generation to generation in the oral tradition. As Arnold has explained this to me—the stories take on a life of their own, and they are constantly evolving as each generation adds their own ideas and inferences to them.

Arnold Isbister lives with his family in Saskatchewan, Canada. His family's heritage is Plains Cree. The name Moshum means Grandfather and Kokum means

Grandmother, and it is often the case that numerous Moshums and Kokums co-exist as generations overlap. Arnold has shared anecdotes where this occurrence has resulted in comical misunderstandings.

As Arnold's publisher—it has been very important to us that the voices of the people in his stories are not changed. Nor did we wish to change Arnold's voice...for the sound of these stories when read aloud is resonant and full of cultural and historical lyricism. These stories originate in one family, but have universal relevance.

So please read, listen, enjoy and learn. It is with great pride that we present *Stories Moshum & Kokum Told Me* to our readers....

Stacey Lynn Newman
Wingate Press

THE AUTHOR - age two or three years

Stories

Moshum & Kokum

Told Me

Wake of the Missionary

"Who are these people, Moshum?" Warren asked.

"Friends and relatives...most of them gone now."

An uneasy silence followed. Warren's grandfather continued to gaze at the photographs, one by one, just about all of them were black and white. Warren watched his Moshum flipping methodically through the tattered pictures.

Sometimes Moshum would display a look of recognition, or a smile, sadness. Once in a while he would grunt with a shake of the head. Warren's grandfather was not just looking at photographs, he was visiting the past as well. Moshum looked at a one picture for a long time. Warren stood up, looked over Moshum's shoulder and saw a typical family scene from years ago. Scanning each face, he saw a tall man in the background with deep scars across and around his nose.

"What happened to him, Mosh?" he asked, pointing to the man.

"Smallpox," Moshum was serious.

"Is that like chicken pox?"

"Much worse. To the white people, it was less serious. To the natives, it brought great sickness and death. Those who did not die were left with terrible scars all over their bodies and faces."

"They died?"

"Oh, yes. Millions died, and not just from smallpox, but from the flu, whooping cough, measles, and sometimes even a cold could bring death. Our people didn't have resistance to these new diseases the explorers and missionaries brought here. When white people first came across the oceans, they did not realize what they brought with them—and neither did the natives.

"From the first meeting, the sickness spread like a fire across the dry prairie. There was no stopping it. How do you stop something you cannot see? When it was finished in one region, it found its way to another, and another. You know?" Moshum formed a circle with his hands. "And when it had completed its journey, it came back again—this happened three times. Three, maybe four times, the sickness came to visit and in its path it left great sorrow and suffering."

Moshum was shaking his head.

"You know, Warren, back then, you could go to any village, any tribe and you would hear the crying...the grief. There was a great sadness across this land and nobody was left untouched. When the explorers and missionaries came back many years later, this time to settle, they found villages empty and whole tribes gone— they were gone forever. When they met those who had survived, they knew from the scars that sickness had been there. Some of the settlers were good, they helped—some didn't care.

"People thought differently back then, you know. Some thought we did not have souls or spirits. Then there were those who decided they were going to civilize us and save our souls. These same people, in their righteousness, brought more pain, more sadness, and more sickness as they travelled west."

There was a pause as Moshum shifted his weight in the chair.

"You know...before the white people came to the west, especially the missionaries, the people knew of them already. Their coming was prophesied in a legend told from one generation to the next. The legend says that a warrior was out alone on the plains when the morning started to come. He was happy for the bountiful food, the many herbs and plants, and the good health of his family. A smile came to his face as he thought of his good fortune.

"Still smiling, he looked to the east where the Morning Star was—and from which direction all good things come. Looking for the Morning Star, he noticed a dark spot in the sky that seemed to get bigger. On the horizon, he saw a dark figure that was moving funny— and was getting closer. The warrior thought *this must be how Death moves* when he saw how slow and unnatural its movements were. It was now close enough that he could tell it was dressed like a missionary—all in black. This stranger's face was pitted with terrible dark holes.

"Stopping, the stranger asked *Who are you?*

"*I am Warrior of the Plains and I have many Tribes,* answered the warrior.

"*I have never heard of you,* said the stranger, *or of these Tribes. Who are they?*

"The warrior explained, *They are my people and are like me. We roam the Plains that are many days long and many days wide.* He then asked the stranger, *Who are you?*

"*I am Smallpox*, the stranger answered.

"*I have never heard of you. Where do you come from, what do you do, and why are you here?* asked the Warrior.

"*I come from far away, across the Great Waters,* replied the stranger. *I am one with the white men—they are my people. Sometimes I travel ahead of them. Sometimes I lurk behind. But, I am always with them, in their camps, in their houses, no matter where they move.*

"*What do you do?* the Warrior asked again.

"*I bring death and sickness,* Smallpox replied. *My breath causes children to wither like young plants in the spring snow. I bring destruction, sadness and grieving. No matter how beautiful a woman is, once she has looked at me, she becomes ugly. To men, I bring not death alone, but the destruction of their children and the blighting of their wives. Everyone in my path will linger in their suffering, and no people who have looked on me will ever be the same.* With that, the stranger and Warrior parted, each going their own way. Our world was never the same." Moshum ended.

Looking down, he said, perhaps as an afterthought, "You know, Warren, I read somewhere that 100 million North and South American Natives died as a result of these diseases. 100 million people—an Armageddon!"

The Warrior in the Woods

Warren was up at 6:30 this morning—his Moshum had been up since 5; a whole hour and a half already. Waking up early was becoming easier. With no electricity, no television, and the closest neighbours miles away, going to sleep early was no problem. Up here in the winter, the darkness came early and left late. This morning was no exception. Looking out through the frost-filled window he could see it was still dark, a darkness heavy with cold, he thought, and shivered.

His small, cast iron bed, with its mattress smelling of smoked hide and sweet grass, was in one corner of the one-room cabin. Looking to the table underneath another ice-cloaked window, he could see Moshum sitting in the orange glow of the lamp. Highlighted in orange and yellow, wrinkles emphasized by shadows, his face reminded Warren of a famous portrait he saw in some school book—Rembrandt, he figured.

Mosh had been looking at some old photos and, holding one now, he seemed lost in thought, lost in memories. With his glasses balanced at the end of his nose, Moshum stared intensely at the grey figure in the photograph. Remembering a story from a long time ago as a child, a smile slowly came to his face. Warren was standing next to him now in his long-johns and moccasins. Looking at the picture, Warren could make out an older woman with hair in braids and her hands down on the shoulders of a small child at her feet.

"Who's that, Mosh?" Asked Warren.

"That's my Kokum, my grandmother," he said, "and that's me there." pointing to a skinny kid squinting in the sunlight.

"Geez Mosh, you look like a nerd!" Warren remarked, laughing.

"Yeah, guess I did," his eyes sparkling with memories. He became silent for a moment, his smile frozen. Tapping at the photo with his finger, he said in an almost sacred whisper, "You know... I remember a true story Kokum once told me...around the time this was taken." Still tapping at the black and white picture, he looked up and asked, "Do you believe in dreams, Warren?"

"I dunno...I never thought about it." With a question on his face, he continued, "But some dreams are just silly."

"Well, at the time, they may not have meaning, but later on when you're older, they might. My grandmother was a strong believer in dreams. Every morning, she would ask us about our dreams, then after thinking about them, she would advise us on what to do. I think she did this because one time long ago, when she was young, she had a scary dream and didn't pay heed. As she put it back then; she was too young to take anything seriously. But as it turned out, two years later, the dream became real. The dream had been a warning. She was younger than you at the time, probably around ten years old.

"She'd had dreams before, but not like this one. She says it was like being awake, thinking and feeling things as if she were there. As she slept in the tipi, she kept waking up from short dreams—really short, like pictures. She would recall a yellow sun in one, trees in another, and voices from another. The dreams would startle her awake. She had sweat on her forehead. She would feel around with her hands, feeling the buffalo robe, feeling the sides of the tipi, reassuring herself that she was awake.

"She then fell into a deep sleep, and she could remember thinking, *I'm dreaming now, I'm awake as another person, but I'm in a dream of my other self sleeping over there.* Soon, she was in place of brilliant white. Her feet felt the cold of the snow, her cheeks felt the wind, and her eyes watered from the crispness of the air. As she blinked, she became aware of trees around her— white, tall trees and a sun, a yellow sun. To her left, she saw white owls, and they were looking at each other. As they continued to talk, she began to understand them. They talked of her uncle, Long Fox. They then stopped and looked directly at her, and she knew in her heart something bad was going to happen to her uncle.

"While looking at the owls, she could hear footsteps crunching in the snow, and she became aware of somebody to her right. Scared to look, but unable to stop herself, she turned and saw a tall, handsome Warrior on a white horse, his face in war paint, and a white robe over his shoulders. The white horse had war paint on it too, and there was a shield with a white Buffalo skull on it.

"She looked and realized that the Warrior was her uncle, Long Fox, and at that moment, he turned and saw the owls. Kokum knew that Uncle understood the owls, and understood their warning, but his pride clouded his reason...for he was a Warrior. Not taking heed of the warning, not taking this sign seriously, Kokum knew Uncle was doomed.

"As she realized this, one of the owls came swooping down at her, and she awoke. Terrified, she sat in silence. After calming down, she called to her mother, but everyone was asleep.

"Thinking to herself later, she felt foolish at how scared she had become. *I will tell Uncle next time he comes,* she told herself, as she lay back down. She never did see her uncle again. About two years after that, a visitor came and brought bad news. Her uncle, riding his favourite white horse, had gone on a horse raid by himself and never returned.

"But, before he left, he recounted a strange dream to this visitor. He said he had dreamed of having a conversation with owls, and of wanting to talk with his niece about something. He had laughed about the dream and thought it was foolish.

"My Kokum turned away crying at this point and never retold the dream to her parents. It was to me in later years that she told this story when she became old, and it was with sadness and guilt in her voice. She used to say that sometimes, when she went out to collect herbs and bark in the winter, that she would hear the owls calling her—and she would hear a wind, a horse breathing with hooves crunching the snow—but there was nothing there. Just a memory I guess, like a wind that comes and goes. I sure miss my grandparents and their stories.

"We're like that, you know. Our lives. We as people will come and go like a wind or as a spark spiralling upwards from a fire. Life is short but memories are long.

"This is why I tell you these stories, so that you may pass them on when you are older. Maybe you will have grandchildren to retell these to? "

"I don't think so Mosh, I hate girls. They're no fun!"

"Just wait, your thinking will change. You know, I remember...."

Northern Lights

"Oooooh...." Michelle exhaled into the cold, with the air recording her breath, "It's coooold!" she exclaimed, her teeth chattering. "Hey Warren, remember that singer we heard on the radio last night? Listen to this...." With her chin and teeth vibrating uncontrollably, she drawled out, "Hooooooooome o-o-o-n d-d-da r-r-a-a-a-ange." Both began giggling, thinking about it, visualizing the scene. They burst out laughing. Across the flat white snow and through the clear air you could probably hear them a mile away, accompanied with the ping-ping and rattle of the harness on the horses.

It was cold, but comfortable as Michelle sat between Moshum and Kokum with a blanket drawn up around her. Warren, six years old, her younger brother, sat on Moshum's lap as he helped to hold the reins for the team of horses. These long, flat ropes of leather connected to the horses' mouths—King and Queen they were called—

controlling which direction they went. This was an adventure to the kids, but still routine and necessary in certain tasks for the grandparents. Although the outside world had its highways, cars, trains; here on the reserve, technology had been suspended in time and action. Michelle thought of these things as their laughter subsided.

The city has a lot of things including noise, pollution, she thought, *but here you have something you can't make, The Time Machine.* The thought came to her as an image flashed in her mind precipitated by a feeling. *Another world, another time,* she mused. As the horses pulled the sleigh, their swishing, thumping of hooves, steady blowing of their nostrils produced a rhythm, *like an orchestra,* she thought. She began to tap the tips of her fingers to her knee in rhythm, accompanied, accentuated by the metal of the harness.

She realized this routine or something like it had probably inspired those old singers Moshum listened to. Hmmm, she murmured as she hummed. Her senses were now keenly aware of movement and sound, she noticed little plumes of vapour, wispy fingers of heat rising from the horses. Opening her mouth, she tasted the cold while watching these fingers elongate then disappear in the blackness of the night. Her eyes drawn upwards, she could see little pinpricks of light in the sky. A fantasy enveloped her as she imagined someone on the other side of this sheet of blackness poking holes into it so some light could come through. Moving her eyes across this blanket of stars, she also recalled Moshum telling her of one of their old chiefs who they called Ahtahkakoop—a blanket of stars....*a nice name*, she contemplated. Thinking of this, she continued her observation, finally resting her eyes on the North. Faintly at first, she saw ghost-like waves emerge from this blanket then start to cover then consume (she fantasized) everything. Frozen in her stare, she assumed at the onset these were vapours coming from the horses, and then fearfully understanding it was happening over her—it overwhelmed her! She grabbed Kokum's arm instinctively as the waves began to dance becoming alive in their metamorphosis from colour to colour.

"Wow! Northern lights!" she exclaimed, mouth staying open. "Will they hurt us?" she asked.

"No, not if you respect them." Kokum replied reassuringly.

Michelle watched now in incredible delight as the lights played the sky, exploding one colour into another changing the intensity and hue all around it. Suddenly, directly above her, they opened up—or split apart in purple, red, indigo, emerald green, summer blue. A vortex made of moving changing colours created an illusion of an endless chasm that she would fall into. She held Kokum's arm tighter as she looked away. Regaining her composure and courage, she lifted her head to the sky again.

"Awesome!" she screamed.

"Shhhhh," Kokum warned.

"Look Kokum, they're alive!" With these shrills of
wonder, the waves seemed to respond in a sudden shift
of colour replying with an audible whoosh. There
seemed an electric prickly feel to the air now as Michelle
became scared.

"I told you!" Kokum stated in a hushed authoritative
tone, "Now, be quiet."

"Yeah!" Warren whispered. Moshum had by this time
halted the team to take in the spectacle. He didn't say
anything; just sitting, his head upward and a soft stream
of fog spiraling to the sky. In the foreground, King and
Queen were at attention and motionless, like royal
soldiers, they were making the only sounds with their
deep breathing as beads of snow and miniature icicles
formed around their nostrils. All watched in awe as the
dance continued, encompassing everything overhead
and the vastness of the surrounding plains isolated them
in wonderment.

With an insight beyond her ten years, Michelle reflected,

"We're just a speck in this display of Mother Earth. We are only here because she tolerates us." After what seemed forever, yet strangely brief, the dancing lights began to diminish retreating further to the north.

The silence was broken by Warren's extended hushed "Woooowwww." They all looked at one another, smiled then looked back up at the sky. Another silence full of amazement ensued. Still gazing at a shrinking ribbon of light in the north, Michelle asks, "What was that about respect Kokum?"

Still gazing at the sky, Kokum takes a long time answering, "You saw those lights?" more a question than a statement, "and did you think they were alive?" she asked, looking at Michelle.

"Yeaaah," replied Michelle, uncertain of the question.

Moshum begins to speak, "The old people from a time so long ago, we cannot count or remember, say that these lights ARE alive. Alive, not like you, and me, but in spirit. Some say they are warriors still doing battle, others say they are departed souls lighting the way for those to follow while others claim they (pointing skyward) are celebrating, dancing in honour of someone or that something good has been done. I prefer the last one, I'm sure there are more stories with different explanations.

"One thing common to all is to respect them in silence when they honour you with their dance. It's like a grand pow-wow where you wouldn't be shouting or yelling; at least that's the way it used to be. The elders say, if you call out to them, whistle or sing, the spirits will come down to take you away. That's why Kokum was telling you to hush. I'm sure nothing would have happened in your case because you didn't know and there was no disrespect."

"Oh....I didn't know Mosh."

"My point exactly, Michelle. Are you listening too Warren?"

"Yeah!" Warren says...still in awe of the spectacle.

"Okay...good....now you know. So, let me tell you a story; a short one but long in learning....A few generations ago, there was a young boy hard in his heart and not right in his thinking. Every new generation has kids as such although, there seems to be more nowadays. I think parents don't control or discipline their young anymore, just letting them roam around doing whatever they want. We were dirt poor but our parents were still parents so having no money is no excuse. Words, story telling, hugs don't cost anything. Anyway...where was I? Oh yes...

"This one boy seemed at odds with everyone and everything, always fighting in words, never listening, no respect and always making fun of others' bad luck, or misfortunes as they say. Many knew of his behavior and knew better than to be with him. But, there were other kids who played with him for the excitement, not knowing what was to happen. Maybe they didn't do what he did or copy him—but they were still watching, not stopping his actions. They were looking the other way when he spoke to his elders in harsh unkind words. Smiles would come over their faces as they watched in amusement when he would get into trouble or they saw people not knowing what to do or say when they became angered or embarrassed. To me, this group doing nothing were the worst because they knew better and only stayed with him for entertainment—something new, exciting and always not good was happening. But they didn't care, they weren't scared of what reaction might occur since they were innocent.

"So, this one cold day in the winter when the moon was full all were gathered around a campfire for talking and storytelling. This same story came to be told but was met with laughing and scoffing from this particular young man. *Aaaaahhh!* He yelled. *Do you believe this foolishness? Are you going to listen to these old men? These old men who can't even see us across this fire or even remember our names? Huh!* He screamed as the elders looked downward in sadness. *Don't you know why they tell these stories? It's to scare us so they can control us like puppies!*

"No. One of the elders said. *We tell these stories so that you may gain in knowledge. We give you our wisdom and experience so you don't repeat our mistakes and suffer or become harmed.*

"*Aaaahh!* He screamed again pointing to the elder. *Don't listen to him! I will show you. Come with me to the field outside our village where I will prove myself.* He said while his group smiled. Stomping out as his friends followed, he did not notice footsteps of the others so he stopped and turned. Still seated, the elders and most of the village gazed at the fire within the gathering circle, saying nothing. *Cowards! You are ALL cowards!* He yelled pointing around. This was very bad, very bad to point and accuse. But none arose to confront him, instead letting him continue.

"He motioned to his group and they followed him. Coming into the bare field, you could see their shadows on the snow cast by the full moon. To the north, you could see dimly a ribbon of dancing spirits as they moved slowly and darkly. The young man then began to dance imitating in a bad way the spirits' slow motion. From his mouth came a make-up song with whistling sounding like an elk, as his group looked on and at each other in amazement and amusement. Nothing happened so they started to laugh and join in. Wild, bad like wolverines, they continued without caution, not fearing anybody in their craziness.

"Suddenly, as you saw tonight (reminds Michelle and Warren of the northern lights) a cloud of dark colours appeared quickening in its movement and cackling with sound. A bright flash sparked the sky and when they could see again the group saw in fear, the young man rising to the sky. Watching, frozen there with their eyes growing white, they could see him getting smaller, his screams getting weaker, then...nothing. His group began to panic, they couldn't move and one-by-one, in terror, they disappeared into the lights—then the blackness. Except one—one who was struck dumb without voice or sound. They say he was left so that he could tell the story, warn others with his pictures instead of his words."

"So...this is the story of the Northern Lights. What do you think it means...what does it teach you?" Moshum asked Michelle and Warren.

"Be respectful. Don't say bad things to people." Warren answers.

"Right...how about you Michelle?" asks Moshum.

"Hmmmm...yes, but I also think that it means that respect should go farther. Not just to people and things like the Northern Lights and Mother Earth, but to what others believe in. Because we don't believe or understand in something, or someone...we should not make fun of it."

"Very good. Now...let's get home to a nice warm fire. Giddy-up," he says as the horses jerked the sleigh to a start. Soon they crossed the endless fields coming to the pines and emerging from around the bend was the old house. "Look!" Moshum pointed. "Someone's home, there's a light in the window."

By home he meant his home, his house, which was home to everybody.

Reflections of Life

The Plains Cree:

A Gallery of Works

by

Arnold J. Isbister

"A Meeting"

"Healing Ceremony"

"My Hands"

"The Conversation"

"Sacred Ground"

"The Red Fence"

"Wake of the Missionary"

"Warrior in the Woods"

"We-Sah-Kay-Chak (The Trickster)"

"Going Home"

"Mrs. J"

"Adam & the Little People"

"Up-See-So Ai-See-Neh-suk"

The Little People

"A-Pis-Chee-Nee-Suk"

"Hey Mo-shum, do you believe in fairies, leprechauns and stuff like that?" asked Chelsea abruptly, staring outside.

Moshum looked at her, studying her as she sat there with a slight frown over her eyes. He followed her eyes through the window to the distant birch and pine in the horizon. "I'm not sure. I never saw any and I don't know of anybody who has. But, I know of a few people who said they saw or heard the *Little People*."

"Really! You've seen them? What are Little People?"

"No, I haven't seen them myself. I said I know of others who said they have."

"Little People." Chelsea whispers to herself. "So, what are they?" she asks in a demanding tone. "How big are they? Are they bad, do they eat kids?"

"No, no, no...they don't eat anybody, that's a *Wetigo*. And how big or bad they are I don't know either. What I heard...."
Chelsea interrupts, "Boy, you don't know too much do you Moshum and what's a Witobo?"

"Wee-teh-go," Moshum says phonetically, "and it's a cannibal spirit...."

"Wow, tell me about him...where is he, who is he?"

"Listen, quit talking." A hush ensued as Moshum bent down looking into her eyes. "You have to be respectful when you ask questions. That means no interrupting especially when there's a story being told. You should be a little more like your big brother, Warren. There's an old saying Chelsea...*you hear but you don't listen, you look but don't see, you touch but don't feel.* Do you know what that means? It means you're not paying attention to what's being said or shown. So, do you want me to continue?" he states more than asks because he knows her answer already.

"Sorry Mosh," with a practiced pose and puppy eyes she asks, "can you finish the story?" She knows she's acting but this always works with the grandparents, as it does now. Realizing with a fear, though, that she had something that could be lost now she becomes anxious, pleading, "Pleeease Moshum."

Smiling, knowing full well the outcome of this scene and with a voice inferring defeat, he says, head bent down, "Oooookay...."

In the background he could hear Kokum with disgust in her chuckle, *Get on with the story you old horse.* She turns to smile at them both, towel in hand she goes to the black and beige trim stove. She lifts the stove lid to put in more wood, the fire illuminates her face revealing a new profile and casting a shadow onto the ceiling. Stoking the flames, sparks dance upward with the embers awakening in a crackle and pop.

Seeing now with insight she remembers Moshum's quote—look but don't see. Intense, focused, she becomes aware of all the oranges, yellows, shadows being played on the walls and ceiling. Even the darkness has colour she notices when her eyes dilate, taking in the deep blues, greens and purples of the shadows. She drinks in this potion of colours, getting lost in the kaleidoscope. A hum envelops her as real sounds cease and thoughts become audible. In the distance, a familiar echo grabs hold as she realizes her name being called. Concentration broken (or redirected) she turns to the source seeing Moshum's lips moving but no voice like a dubbed videotape. Snapping out of it she hears, "Chelsea?"

"What?" she replies in a monotone.

"The story...do you want to hear the story?" Moshum is looking at her inquisitively with head at a slight tilt.

"Oh, yes...yes. Sorry again Mosh, I was looking at Kokum. I just remembered that I don't think I've ever seen Kokum without her apron."

"Aaaaahh...yeah. Anyway....about the Little People. I've heard a lot of stories and there's no clear explanation of them or what they are about or what they mean. Some say they are there for comfort and support while others say they bring bad luck or are a premonition of things to come.

"I remember an old lady living by herself north of this lake. Her husband of many years had passed on and we, (Kokum and I) would drop in to visit. We would bring her things to eat, clean her house and cut wood for her when she was running low 'cause she was really old. Others had told us of hearing the laughter of small kids, footsteps, even rustling of bushes when they would visit, but could see no children. So, this one time we went, we decided to be aware of everything around us and to ask her about these stories. Getting there, I started with chopping some wood while Kokum went inside to greet the old lady we called Mrs. J."

Seeing a bit of confusion on Chelsea's face, Mosh explained, "through the years, because of her original long name, *Crosses the River*, it had been abbreviated to simply Mrs. J." Sitting toward the edge of the chair, he places his elbows on his knees, clasping his hands together, fingers intertwining in a dovetail.

Continuing, he says, "As Kokum gets to the door we both hear movement in a nearby bush. At the door now, her eyes toward the rustling, she becomes startled when without knocking on the door, Mrs. J yells *Pee-ta-kway'—Come in!* So Kokum goes in, after a hug and some pleasantries, they sit down on some old chairs, the paint chipping away now. The table is just some grey boards nailed together on top of four rickety legs and it sways when you put any weight on it.

At this point, Kokum interjects with a non-verbal nod from Moshum to continue the story in her own words. She begins without hesitation as if the moment was choreographed. "Uh huh...Sitting there I saw across the dark room a slab of bannock freshly baked leaning at an angle on the stovetop against the stovepipe. I could see through the dim light there was also an old red lard pail full of tea. I asked *Were you expecting someone?* Mrs. J replies *Yes, I knew some one would come today.* (Don't forget, Chelsea, this is all spoken in Cree, but I'm translating and sometimes you can't describe in English, the 'feel' of a conversation). I knew from her words, eyes and the air around her that she said this without question. Mrs. J adds, *the 'little ones' told me to get ready for visitors today.*

"So I nodded as if this is completely normal. She gets up slowly and pours me some tea, breaks off some bannock—still hot and hands me the homemade butter and jam. Mmmm...this was good. So, while we nibble at our bannock and muskeg tea, we talk. Usually it was a time to catch up on what was going on 'out there', who was doing what, who married, who died, where was 'so-and-so' and so on.

"With time getting short, I told her I had come to help in her cleaning. She was pleased with this as she was having a hard time with her knees and back. I was told what she wanted done, her old finger bent with arthritis pointing to the different areas. Finishing the front, which was all kitchen, living room and bedroom, I went to a small back room used for storage. This hadn't been cleaned for a long time so I was there the longest. Kneeling on a floor of rough boards, I looked up to see Mrs. J silhouetted by the only window with its glass cracked and dirty. You could tell there was a film of smoke on the glass that gave it a dull blue colour and when the light came through it you could see these little specks of dust floating in ghostly fingers of light.

"Anyway, kneeling there I could see her motioning, talking in a whisper to someone I couldn't see. With that sun coming in, I couldn't see in the shadows, just a dark blur but more oval like an egg—a dark blob that was not natural. The way it moved too was weird, like when you see something at the corner of your eye, which you can't see but you can tell it's slowly moving? Well, anyway, kneeling on the floor, squinting my eyes, I thought somebody must have come in, maybe Moshum but he's not small or looks like an egg—right?"

"Right!" Chelsea agrees, smiling, noting he's pretty big too.

"So, I sit up like this," Kokum stretches her back straight up, "and ask...*Who's there? Did somebody come in?* Mrs. J turned quickly and I can hear scampering, you know like kids or cats running away. I feel spooked then, not really scared but a sense of something not right, something unnatural. Looking but not seeing, all I could make out was small dark figures moving to the back of the stove and behind where there was wood piled up against the wall. I stand up and follow the noise with my eyes but already they were gone—just like that...poof. No sounds, now nothing. Mrs. J and I stare at each other for a long time then she slowly smiles almost like she's relieved. *Did you see them?* She asks quietly. I think, replaying what I saw, then tell her, *I don't know Mrs. J, I saw something. What was it, what were they?* I asked, by this time my voice is trembling. I start to notice I'm shaking all over and my legs are weak. *Sit down.* The old lady says, which I do, using that rickety old table as a crutch. It's funny how you think when you're in shock, cause I'm thinking to myself, I hope this table holds me or else we're all on the floor. Mrs. J continues to smile and I know she feels good about this, about me seeing something. *I thought maybe in my old age, I am starting to see things that are not there.* She states with a long sigh. *Well, I saw something.* I tell her.

"*I call them up-see-so ai-see-ne-suk, those People who are Little.* She goes on, telling me in Cree. *They have been around for countless generations and were talked about in whispers. My parents and their grandparents knew about them but few talked for fear of being seen as 'not right' or, crazy. They are a myth, a real thing without proof except for those of us who have experienced them. But these are just words and people can take or leave them, mostly leaving them 'cause they want proof—something more than a story. A long time ago, our ancestors were more open because that is how our history was passed on, by mouth. Nowadays with radio, telephone, picture shows, books, it seems we are not happy with just words and talking. We have to see things—even we are not satisfied with talk. Why are the same stories spoken a long time ago more important if we read them in a book or hear them over radio or television? I ask myself this in my old age. I fear to ask our young because they will have too many answers. Anyway, my dear one, I am straying. Ai-see-ne-suk?* she asks herself. *I don't know. Some say they are good, some say, they bring bad things. For myself, they bring company when I am lonely, the days seem longer when you are alone. When they come they talk to me, to each other and always in good spirits. I have comfort in hearing them, they are like little kids especially when playing games. I hear their laughter reminding me of lost memories when I was a child, a time I forgot when I grew up. This makes me happy to feel young again in my old age.* Then she waves her hand over her body, *you see this old bent body? I cannot run, jump like in my childhood. It is only with memories I can do what I used to do.*

"She sits there a long time lost in her thoughts. I don't want to break the silence, so we sit quietly gazing at the darkness where the Little People disappeared. Almost at the same time, I was asking myself, as if she was reading my mind, she says, *they look funny. They are small, like little dolls and they move so quick. Do you watch the squirrels in the trees? That's what they remind me of.*

"I ask then, *What colour are they because I've heard others say...*

"Mrs. J interrupts. *Colour? I don't know. I never looked at them to see their colour. They seem perfect, they have excitement like children but faces of those older, like adults. The ones I see...their eyes are dark, not dark, as in something bad as if they know everything. You get lost in their eyes but it's not scary, it brings a comfort like when you look at your parent's eyes and you feel and know they would do anything to protect you. Do you know what I mean?* Mrs. J asks.

"I knew exactly what she meant." Kokum says and Chelsea, after some reflection knew this also. Chelsea, now hypnotized with fantastic images, wonders aloud to herself, "how big are they?"

"I asked her that too." Kokum replies as she sat there, "and Mrs. J said, *they are real small, about this high,* as she lowered her outstretched hand to below her knees. *They are slim in body with large heads and short necks. Some seem to have no neck at all. Their legs, arms are also slender without muscle, like children and they move with the quickness of small animals. Their fingers* as she remembers *were longer, more delicate, like those of a young woman and those eyes...*Mrs. J's voice fades away as she lives the memory." Kokum repeats, acting out the scene as her tone becomes hushed, solemn. In her concentration, she becomes Mrs. J as Chelsea watches, anticipating a secret is going to be revealed.

Kokum continues Mrs. J's description, "*those eyes...are deep, like looking into a well where at first you see nothing. After you stare awhile, you begin to see reflections or ripples of waves or moving water—their eyes are timeless as if they have lived forever. And purple, I see dark purple with waves of dark transparent blue in them*...then Mrs. J here almost shocked as I see her face in surprise as she turned to me. She asks me *you know what?...What?* I ask.

"Mrs. J continues revealing to herself as if I'm not there, *there are no young ones among them...they are all old. Maybe not in years, but adults or grown-ups who know so much*, she shakes her head trying to understand—trying to explain. She remained silent contemplating why this would be, then answered herself. *They have always been, they are forever.* With this, she tells me she has grown tired so we excuse ourselves to leave. We said our goodbyes closing the door when I remembered my broom and went back to the cabin.

"Before reentering, I heard Mrs. J asking, *how old are you?* Then I heard a reply in a small voice, *Tonight while we look at the stars...we will tell you a story.* I stopped, and then turned away not wanting to interrupt or break their secret talk. While we loaded up everything onto the wagon, we noticed little trails with footprints all around the house through to the nearby willows and back deeper into the pines. There were a lot of them. It's funny how you can see so much when you know what it is.

"A lot of people, mainly trappers come across these footprints, smaller than a baby's, deep in the forests, some claim they have even discovered miniature villages, but nobody there.

"Can you imagine that?" Kokum asks, continuing, "Little tipis in a clearing deep in the forest with small little fires. Smoke coming up from them, maybe even pots on them with something cooking. I wonder what they eat?"

Kokum, still sitting, turns to the window, her focus on the far-away pines hazed in purple and deep blues.

Chelsea comes up beside her, taking her hand, she presses her head onto Kokum's shoulder. Kokum reaches over with the other hand caressing her hair then turns to whisper. With her mouth close to Chelsea's ear, she could feel her warm breath as she ended, "So...next time you hear a rustling in the forest, stop. Look around...you may see...the Little People."

ADAM & THE LITTLE PEOPLE

"I remember another story my own Kokum told me," states Moshum matter-of-factly, "but this one is different, kind of strange."

"Strange?" Chelsea asks, "How is it strange Moshum?"

"Well, listen, learn and you'll see." He replies with his index finger pointing to his ear then with two fingers to his eyes. "Strange is when a thing can't be described or explained but it feels weird. One person might find it weird but another might think it normal too. Yep, strangeness is strange!" jokes Moshum with a sideways glance and quizzical look at Chelsea.

She says in wonder, "I guess this is strange."

Moshum becomes silent and then solemn. Slowly, sitting up, crossing his arms and then crossing his legs after stretching them out, he begins. "I remember my great grandmother who we call Kokum, telling me of a young man she once knew. He was tall, slim, nice-looking and had something about him so you never forgot his face. One time at a Sun Dance my Kokum pointed him out and I never forgot. I was a young child like you, at the time. This was before airplanes, and cars were new then, none were around here. You wonder why I mention this about airplanes, but this will become clear after and you will know it's important—not just an old man rambling away in his talking. Anyway, this young man, we'll call Adam, seemed to be a loner as I watched him walk. No one stopped to talk to him, in fact, it seemed to me that people avoided him as I watched him come across the field towards us. I became scared not knowing why this feeling came over me as I crept behind my Kokum.

He stopped and then he talked to my Grandmother for a little while being pleasant in all ways and showing respect. It seemed that there was much wisdom and knowledge in him as he spoke, despite his very young years, which were only twelve. All this time, while they spoke, it came to me that my grandmother not once had lifted her head to look him in the eye. Everything was nice; there was no anger, there were no bad words, no visible reason to treat him in this manner, they bid their goodbyes as he went on his way in his fashion. He held himself straight, his chin out with his eyes not dancing about to see if others were paying attention to him." Moshum postures himself up as his memories come alive.

He continues. "I was reminded of our proud Chiefs from a time forgotten as Adam proceeded on his journey. I call it a journey because he walked with purpose and without that restless energy of youth that you might have expected him to have. His steps were measured, definite and straight. I kept watching him through that fateful day."

Pausing, he now slips to the floor and Moshum relaxes. His voice changes, becoming monotone as he says to himself, "I felt sorry for him...," catching himself, he restates with conviction, "the more I watched him that day, the more I felt sorry for him."

"Why, Moshum?" Chelsea asks quietly, so as not to break the atmosphere.

"Adam did not seem to have any friends, or enemies. Twelve years old, with nobody accepting you or admitting your presence must hurt. But, he didn't seem to mind or he hid it well. Towards the night as people went to their tipis, in the twilight, I sat beside Kokum at our fire. There were a lot of questions in me as I watched the flames and saw the sparks become stars in the sky. Having watched Adam that day, I had become fearful then depressed as I thought of his life. I did not understand my connection to this boy. Feeling my silence, Grandmother asked me in Cree, *Nosim (grandson), what bothers your spirit?* I tell her and she replies *there is no need to hurt yourself with these feelings. Nothing will change in this village. Our village people see Adam, his story, his life as so strange. Most fear him. Not that he will do us harm, we are afraid of what he knows. No person likes to talk with him, because he speaks of things to come soon and other things far and distant into the future. He is always right knowing what is to happen tomorrow as well as next year.*

I asked my Kokum *Kokum, why is this so different that we cannot accept him? Aren't there prophets and holy people within our tribe who do and say the same things?* I was trying to find reason. *Yes*, she answered, *but you don't know or understand the real reason.* After much thinking, after wiping away tears from her eyes, she talked of him in the past, as if he had died. *I knew him well, we all knew him well. We played games together.* I was shocked, I could not make sense of what she was saying so to keep things clear. Chelsea, listen to me as I talk as my Kokum did to me that night, in her voice." Moshum looks at Chelsea's eyes as he speaks.

"Adam was a sweet child. Young and old, everyone liked him—his company and his stories. As far-fetched and wild as they were, we enjoyed his presence, and so we nodded in pretend when he spoke of *Little People. Oh yes*, we said, *we know, tell us more.* He would go on about the Little People, their strange ways and the sounds they would make when talking. He could understand all they said. He described their appearance—small with adult faces, eyes like a doll's, their footprints being like a day old baby. He told of their quickness in body as well as in mind, for they were very very smart.

"Then one day, he mentioned he might go away with them and we laughed. The next day we followed him in secret as he went on his early morning walk, he had done this since the snow had begun to melt. When the snow was gone is when he discovered a hill not known to him where he said the Little People lived. We followed in dead silence from bush to bush as he finally came to a stop before a large odd-shaped hill. We waited, smiles on our faces, snickering as children do when they share a secret. Little did we know that this small secret would become a mystery that would affect all of us.

"Adam stood there a long time not doing anything and as time passed, we became silent too. Soon our eyes became lazy, the hillside seemed to move like quicksand and an opening appeared. Adam became quick and shaky in his movements as he began to laugh and speak in a high voice. The edges of his body became softer and inside him everything turned into small, small dots of white and black. Then he disappeared into the hill. Bumps came over our entire bodies and our hairs stood on end—like a porcupine bristling with fear. This scared us even more as we looked at each other. We ran like the deer being chased by wolves. We got home with each of us going into our own tipis where we stayed all day and into the night. The adults had seen our actions and knew something was wrong.

"Adam didn't come back. Later that evening as worries became greater, Adam's father, his relatives and other village warriors scouted the area. With the night becoming darker, they came back questioning our story, saying there was no hill where we said, but only a hole, which they think, was recently dug. After four long days,

68

Adam's parents met with Chief and Council having agreed that the Blackfoot, Sioux had taken him away. Many at this time and before who had lost a son in battle would steal from a warring tribe making that boy their own. And so it went. Memories of him faded. We, who were there seldom spoke about this time for fear we might curse ourselves or those Little People might come for us.

"Time went on, we became adults, had our families, now we have great grandchildren. I was 11 at the time Adam disappeared, he was 10. I was 78 when I saw him again, he was 11.

"I said to my Kokum, *that cannot be so. He should be as old as you, great-grandmother.* My Kokum continued the story of Adam. She told me that during the summer of the falling star, about twelve moons before, Adam came into the village from the North, trembling with cold, being not right in his thinking and talking. He said he had been looking for his home for four months and he was asking why they would move the village so fast in one day and without him. He cried as he talked about his parents, brothers, sisters and friends. My Kokum asked Adam who these people may be and to give her their names in hopes that she might help him. Everybody he named, she knew but they were old now or had departed. She stopped then because a fear choked her words and she couldn't talk—this lasted two days.

"Adam also asked other members of the village, about certain people who looked familiar, but soon nobody would speak to him as they became suspicious, fearful. For food, they gave him enough, along with clothing and robes, but none took him in. Finally, we came together in a circle with Adam in the middle. Some remembered Adam from youth—my Kokum, a younger brother of Adam and another close friend of his. When all questions asked were answered by Adam, with truth and fact, he then asked members of the circle who they were. As the three knowing him personally answered his questions, it became clear that there was a bond here, a secret or secrets only they shared. He cried, they cried as he touched their faces, remembering through his young hands while calling out our names in pain with a deep sadness. They knew, not how or why, but they knew this was the same Adam. My Kokum finished the story, these are her words again Chelsea, the way she told the end of the story to me.

"After two moons, he came to us, bringing tobacco. He wanted us to tell him everything that happened in those sixty-eight years. We did so in twenty-three nights and when finished, he told us in half a night what he did during those past years. He said on that day he was invited by the Little People to go on a trip, which he became so excited about. He entered their dwelling, squinting his eyes as he came into a blinding white room. All around him, his eyes took in reflections, sparkling metals and glass snakes that filled with coloured water. On a wall, he saw a large, black shield that came alive with objects and people of all kinds. This scared him because he could not touch them or hold them as he tried.

"They told him to sit at a spidery chair, as they got ready to go. Sitting into this chair of many silver legs, his eyes were still on the black shield when he noticed his parents become visible like moving drawings that you could walk around. He called out to them with no reply, wondering how they got smaller. Being assured in thought, then voice, they were all fine and what he saw were just copies or drawings of his parents, he rested into the chair. He said he became surrounded in a light and while floating in the air like a hawk gliding he saw our land disappear. Quick as a thought the land became a blue ball with clouds around it then this vanished as other balls of many colours appeared then disappeared. He went through great clouds of north lights and past an exploding sun, then into a pure blackness.

"Soon he was back as he saw the familiar blue ball and sitting again in the spider's chair. He talked to them, asking questions about what he saw, gaining knowledge he could not explain or describe. Our eyes were too small to see his world, so he gave up trying. It's like a dream where colours you never saw exist and there are no words to describe them. In a time it takes a cloud to cross the sky, Adam was out and on his way home eager to tell everyone of his travels. And this is when he found us but everything he knew was gone; even the trees and surroundings always familiar as we age, were not there. Somehow, Adam remained young while we aged. Within the last season, Adam had also aged in wisdom and knowledge well beyond his twelve years. This upsets many people, making them uncomfortable when around him. He doesn't talk to many and very few talk to him. He is like a loon, lost in the winter, looking for water. And that is what my Kokum told me about Adam Chelsea."

"What happened to him, Moshum?" Chelsea asks.

"I never saw him again after that day, neither did anyone else. He disappeared again one evening from the village. He vanished into history and became a story. Some say he went back to the Little People, traveling with them. I do remember on the night that he disappeared, we all saw a falling star come from the East and a short time later saw a light in the West. Remember when I mentioned airplanes, Chelsea?"

"Yes" she replies quietly.

"Well, nowadays, they talk about UFOs as if they're new, but we saw many things in the skies we could not explain way back then. What they describe in the old days now becomes explainable and we understand. Maybe these Little People do exist. Are they part of a greater mystery we will know in the future? A Holy Man of the southern Sioux once said this as he looked upwards into the stars...*I see more than I understand, yet know more than I see.*"

Going Home

Wow, cool! You don't see that in the city, Warren thought as he gazed out the cabin window. Outside, visibility was about two hundred yards and getting worse. Looking at the pine trees, he imagined them groaning in unison as they bent from the wind, their branches reaching out for something. *What are they reaching for?* He wondered.

Maybe there's something out there we don't see...maybe spirits, maybe the people Moshum calls Pakakoos—the legendary people of the forest that were always there, and if you didn't watch it, they would lead you deep into the wilderness to be lost forever.

The Pakakoos were white as the snow with long noses that stuck straight out like branches of a tree, and they didn't talk. Their legs, arms, and hands were gnarled, knotted and bony— with skin like peeling bark. Smiling, they would motion with their hands, beckoning. "This way," they would seem to say..."Come, over here. No, no this way, follow me."

There was a loud banging noise. Warren jumped, he did not expect it; someone was knocking at the door. His heart was loud in his ears, so loud, in fact, that he began to think that it was his heart he had heard and not the door. BANG, BANG! No imagining it this time. He moved further away from the door and closer to where Moshum and Kokum were sitting. They smiled at each other, no surprise on their faces as his stare turned to the door.

"PEETAKWAY! COME IN!" Moshum hollered.

"Don't do that, Moshum!" Warren requested sternly.

"What?" Moshum asked with his smile getting bigger.

"Holler like that!"

"Oh, sorry....what you jumping for? Better go answer the door."

The door opened with a howl, a sheet of snow came dancing in. A figure emerged from the darkness into the orange glow of the interior. Relieved, Warren realized it was Mrs. J, the old lady that lived by herself about two miles down the road.

What the heck is she doing here in this weather? He wondered.

Moshum and Kokum both got up, shook her hand warmly, and motioned for her to sit down. They spoke in Cree as they drank tea and played cards late into the night.

Warren could make out the conversation in bits and pieces from the Cree he knew, and as far as he could tell, they weren't really talking about anything in particular— just small talk. But to him, this was unusual, that this elderly lady would come at night in this weather, then just sit around and talk. He liked Mrs. J, but she didn't speak to children much. Whenever she looked at Warren, it was with a warm smile, more in her eyes than in her mouth. Listening to the wind outside and the hushed voices around the kerosene lamp, he soon drifted off to sleep.

He awoke the next morning to the creaking of the oven door. Glancing sideways, he saw Kokum taking out some bannock, using tea towels as oven mitts. In ten seconds Warren was dressed and at the table eating steaming hot bannock smothered with margarine and homemade strawberry jam. When his hunger was satisfied, his thoughts turned to the events of the night before. Noticing the calm outside, he realized Mrs. J was gone.

"Kokum, where's Mrs. J?"

"She's gone. She left around two in the morning. Hooked up the horses and went home."

"Really? Why did she come in this weather in the first place?" Warren asked, amazed.

"Storms bring back old memories for her, and I guess she likes somebody to talk to at those times."

 "Why? What memories?"

Kokum sat down slowly. With a tea towel in her hands, flour on her face, she began in a whisper. "Well...not long ago, there were Missionary schools. Do you know about them, Warren?"

"Yeah, a bit. I heard that when kids reached a certain age, they were forced to go to school far away from their families and sometimes not come back 'til they were sixteen or eighteen."

"Right. Families had no say, and many would cry when this time came. Some would move away or hide their young when the Indian Agents or priests came around to count the kids they had, and ask how old they were. It was a sad time.

"She was about six when they came around to pick up kids for the Mission School. They took her older brother, Matthew, she adored him. He was about eight at the time, and she was too young to go. Ages for school were a little different then. Her Mom and Dad were heartbroken and she cried many nights for her older brother. She says she remembers so clearly, her brother was put into the back of a truck along with twenty other kids, and as they drove off, the look on his face, scared and sad. Those sad, sad eyes...

"Things slowly returned to normal, although they missed him terribly at Christmas time. During those years, Christmas and Easter were different too, celebrated mainly by the white people, but they were still special times—times for families to gather.

"I think it was close to Easter when word came through the Indian Agent that Matthew was ill, and they wanted his Dad to come and get him. Apparently, all this time, Matthew had been homesick—very homesick, but nobody had thought it was serious.

"So his Dad hurried, got some blankets, some food, and Matthew's favourite horse, a white horse. They were overjoyed, they would all be together again soon. Mrs. J was so happy that her brother was coming back, she knew her Mom and Dad would be like they were before.

"The father left as soon as he could, travelling for two days on horseback, for it was a long ways away. Mrs. J and her mother figured it would be four or five days before they would be home. So, to keep themselves busy, they cooked and baked all the things Matthew loved.

"After reaching the Mission, the father learned that Matthew had passed away—probably from a broken heart. There was no other explanation. Gathering his son's belongings, he immediately set out for home—against the advice of the school.

"They were concerned because winds were picking up and the temperature was dropping. In his grief, Matthew's Dad heard little and was not aware of the weather. A white-out—when everything turns white and you become lost—probably happened. He must have laid down with his son, whose body he had wrapped in blankets and placed on a makeshift travois. With the cold winds beating at him and playing tricks with his mind, they figured he must have taken off his own blanket and wrapped it around Matthew to try and save his poor son's life.

"Mrs. J and her mother were worried. Five days turned to six, then eight. Something must have happened. Maybe Dad had injured himself, or gotten sick. With help from the local priest and other families, they began a search.

"After two days, they found them. In the middle of a prairie they saw a white horse standing alone. Coming closer, they could make out a mound of snow beside the horse. Clearing off the snow, they could see blankets.

Matthew and his dad lay frozen. The boy was wrapped up in blankets, and his father held him in his arms, as if to keep him warm.

"Mrs. J never stopped grieving. Her mother was also never the same, and died a couple of years later, leaving Mrs. J alone. She was brought up by her uncle, who was very loving, but that time still haunts her. She never did go to school.

"She got married young and was happy—with her own kids and, after awhile, grandchildren too. Her husband, Mr. J passed away when he was sixty-five. They'd been married for forty-five years. She's around eighty now."

Warren sat quietly now, facing the window, contemplating. His eyes open, but blind to this world as he envisioned Mrs. J's story.

Moshum Leaves

We had been expecting it—the dreaded phone call—but when it did come, it was still a shock. With all grandparents, the thought is always in the back of the mind as their age becomes more visible, and more so when the grandparent has also developed health problems.

Within the last two years, Moshum had experienced several minor heart attacks along with a stroke. He had come through each with typical optimism—enthusiasm in fact—for the future. In mind he was fine, but sometimes while talking to him I would catch a glimmer of doubt in his eyes as we discussed potential surgery and treatment. To me, and everyone else, it seemed his future was very limited, but he wouldn't acknowledge this. Maybe it was to protect us.

Now he was gone. My father, my children's Moshum,

had left us; each went into their own self and cried. The grandchildren took it especially hard; there was such finality to it.

I remember him telling us, always reminding us, that we all die and it was just another part of life that we could not escape from...part of the journey. I guess those reminders were meant to prepare us for the inevitable—but it still hurt.

He had been laughing—telling a joke or anecdote—when his heart just quit and he fell off a chair onto the floor. Within a matter of seconds, someone had checked his pulse, felt his chest then looked into his eyes. He was gone.

That was fast, I thought, reassuring myself, *which was good...I guess.* Then a smile came to me...yes, I smiled. *That was just like Moshum.* I remembered him smiling, laughing at his own jokes. I suppose for him (and us) this was the best way to go—laughing and telling a story. Yeah, all those stories, so many I can't recall them all, were told to be retold. *As long as I can retell the stories, he's still with us in spirit,* I surmised with a bit of pleasure.

My car was undrivable, so family friends were coming to pick me up in Moshum's car, which was apparently mine now since Kokum didn't drive. It was a warm October day and I sat down to wait. A million memories went through my mind as I flashed through my life with Moshum; wandering, jumping from one age to another. It's funny how memories you don't even know you have come back when you take the time to reflect. We are so busy living, we forget to remember.

An inconsistent stream of images came to me as I sat in reflection, some bringing a tear, others a smile. Recollecting bits and pieces, not dwelling too long on painful events, I intentionally selected the pleasant snapshots to store. I fondly recalled expressions Moshum would mix up such as: "That's the way the cookie bounces," and "That's milk under the bridge" and "Kill two birds with one rock."

He would laugh at himself, and we would join in 'til we

had tears in our eyes. Like the time he went to town and was asked to bring back Reese's peanut butter cups, which he was informed were two small peanut butter wafers. Well, when he came home, Kokum asked, "Where are they?"

Moshum pointed at the two jars of peanut butter on the table.... "Those were the smallest I could find," he said.

He didn't know he was supposed to be looking in the candy section. That was Moshum though, able to laugh at his mistakes or make light of problems, much to the chagrin of Kokum. Her typical response was, "Oh everything will be all right."

I looked out the window and realized it was dark. I had been sitting there, lost in memories, for three hours. The real world was back now, so was the pain. My wife Karen came into the room, "They're here," she said. I got up and got ready to go back home.

Outside, Saskatoon, the night sky was a clear, deep blue with a halo of light on the horizon. The full moon was in the southeast; already brilliant in pale blue with a faint circle forming around it. *A change in the weather*, I thought to myself.

Driving north, with the city well behind us, the sky was even clearer without the layer of light pollution. On the far horizon, we could see an odd flicker—a whisper of colour. "Looks like we're going to have Northern Lights," I said (or did I just think it?) to nobody. I don't even recall if the three of us said any words on that trip.

Fog set in as we neared the river, and got thicker as we approached Blaine Lake. Before we reached Shellbrook, the fog was so thick you couldn't see twenty feet. This lasted for two hours 'til we got home to Moshum's. Finally, approaching the turn-off, I could now see above the blanket of fog.

It was mystical. I briefly forgot why I was there as my eyes encountered the surreal landscape. In every direction all I could see was a moving, swirling cloud of white pierced by pine, ash, and willow trees. The moon in all its glory casts light on this world of white and its inhabitants. The pines looked like skinny pyramids, the ash poplars without leaves were hands reaching upward, and those still with leaves were semi-circular domes. *I am on another planet,* I whispered in my mind, transfixed by the illusion before me.

In the corner of my eye I sensed movement, then looking to the north I saw the lights dancing in the sky. Not quick or jumping but solemn, subtle, sad, I imagined. So beautiful, peaceful with its river of changing colours.

And to the south, an illuminating globe of mystic blue, casting soft shadows of the trees onto the white plane. *I won't see this again,* I mused. The imprint was done, the memory cast in stone.

I drove onward. The pines grew larger, towering over me like cathedrals or castles. I passed them, cutting the fog effortlessly, but the path I forged was swallowed immediately behind me. I left no wake, no trace. Looking in my rear-view mirror, I envisioned that this had meaning, that something was being said, but I couldn't hear it. The pines parted like great sentinels, graciously giving me passage to a clearing.

My lights were off now; I could see more by the moonlight. Through the mist I detected a faint glimmer. Knowing this was a window; I experienced a déjà vu, a feeling that this had happened before. A flood of imagery invaded my mind as I realized I had experienced this, seen this all in my imagination when listening to my Dad and others tell stories.

From all the stories I had made a fantasy world. It was there in my mind, I had just never seen it. They had painted a picture with words that I could see now, a perception I could share. With dawning insight I shook my head in delight, smiling as I came home and to the door.

The house was full; people sitting, standing close to the walls, all very somber. I greeted them; walking around, shaking hands, an occasional hug. It was nice to see them, especially my uncle Clifford, Leona and my nephew Dwayne.

Soon the guests left. There was an uncomfortable silence

while we sat saying nothing. Slowly, my mother and I began to talk—going over details. I learned then that Kokum and Moshum had both known he was too weak to undergo open heart surgery. Both knew, but didn't say, so as to spare the others unnecessary stress and pain. Each waited for the inevitable in their stoic manner. It was typical of how they had always handled the problems life threw at them. Everyone knew, his grandchildren included, but he didn't know they knew.

The next day we made phone calls, some arrangements, plans for the funeral. On my way back to Saskatoon, I stopped in at the funeral home to have a final visit with Moshum. I stood there looking at him. I could hear my heart in my ears, my eyes were filling with tears and, a long ways away, I could hear someone's voice echoing in monotone. The voice told Moshum that everyone was doing fine considering the circumstances; that Michelle and her husband, Lang were coming back and that he was sure happy Moshum had seen his great-grandchildren Donavan and Zachary before he left; that Warren says Hello; and that Chelsea really likes school and Karen still bakes those shortbread cookies he loves. All of them will be seeing him before he left....then I knew the voice had been me.

The day of the funeral was perfect. Beautiful. Full sun, no wind, summer temperatures and a ceiling of deep, sapphire blue you only see in the fall when the sky changes preparing for the cold.

The words came easily, "The autumn of a man's life when he goes to sleep and awakes in the spring." Maybe I had read this somewhere, can't remember. We continued to welcome people, with numb but cordial etiquette, throughout the day. Back home at Moshum's the finality hit us—Moshum was gone. He had left and we wouldn't see him ever again.

I was deeply depressed that evening. We stayed up late, trading, exchanging anecdotes, stories, and facts about Moshum until we became too tired. Every time we talked about him or repeated a quote of his, a flash of him sitting there would trigger even more memories.

My mind raced back to the night I traveled back home

cutting the fog on my journey, but leaving no wake, no evidence. The meaning of that event had escaped me until now. I had a revelation. Although the event had been physical, the action had sparked a philosophical question: Where was I going and what was I leaving? For a few weeks I pondered my revelation, asking myself questions I already knew, but had never answered. I concluded that in writing—retelling his stories—I would keep his memory alive, while also leaving something for my family: His life, his culture. I can hopefully perpetuate not only his memory but also rekindle the philosophy of sharing, and the idea that we are all One. This is why I tell these stories. Although fictional, these stories have a factual basis from which I can paint a story for all to see. They are an allegory of a common man's life, his family, his memories and the legacy he leaves behind for us to take pleasure in, or maybe even learn from. I know Moshum would have approved of this story being included with, and at the end of these stories. "We all die," he would reiterate, "it's part of Life."

Through these stories, he lives on as others before him, his spirit is with us. I can see his face now, reassuring, smiling, saying, *everything will be all right.*

"Yes, Dad, everything's all right," I answer as I put down my pen.

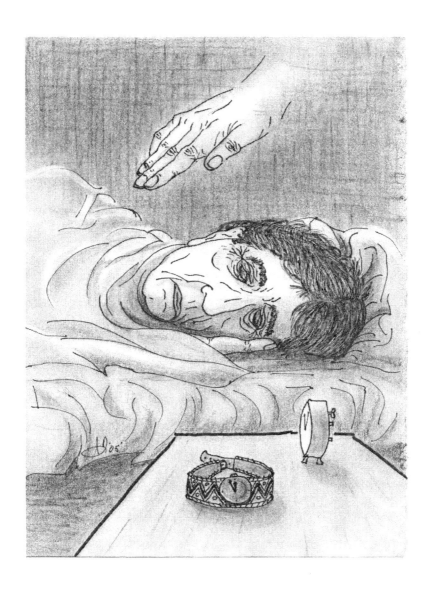

MOSHUM (Paul)

KOKUM (Pansy)

About the Author

"I remember an orange glow from the wood stove fires and the smell of fresh tea or cooked bannock in the air. This was a common scene in most households too since we all shared the same area, conditions, hardships and economy. Everything around us was 'earthy' not only in feel and touch but in color also. Most of us were not high school graduates nor did we have university, many did not even know the English language— this affected the way these stories were told, having or giving a different feel or character to them. The whole environment and time lent itself to storytelling—a major part of our culture. If a person or child somewhere remembers just one of these stories I am happy. Hopefully they will pass it on...or replay it in their minds with smiles on their faces."

Arnold J. Isbister

Arnold J. Isbister lives in Saskatchewan, Canada with his family where he continues to work as a prolific and well known Canadian painter and a writer.